A Feel Better Book

for Little Sports

A FEEL BETTER BOOK
for Little Kids

To all the librarians, champions of little readers
everywhere—*LB & HB*

To my big brother, Greg, who participates in and
loves sports more than anyone I know; and to all
the young sportspeople who try, participate in,
and love sports, win or lose—*SN-B*

Magination Press is a registered trademark of the American Psychological Association. Order books at
maginationpress.org, or call 1-800-374-2721.

Book design by Rachel Ross
Printed by Worzalla, Stevens Point, WI

Library of Congress Cataloging-in-Publication Data
Names: Brochmann, Holly, author. | Bowen, Leah, author. | Ng-Benitez, Shirley, illustrator.
Title: A feel better book for little sports / Leah Bowen, Holly Brochmann ; [illustrated by] Shirley Ng-Benitez.
Description: Washington, DC : Magination Press, [2021] | Series: Feel better books for little kids | Summary:
"A rhyming picture book is about being a good sport, enjoying sports for the fun of it rather than winning, and
appreciating being part of a team"-- Provided by publisher.
Identifiers: LCCN 2020042651 (print) | LCCN 2020042652 (ebook) | ISBN 9781433836947 (hardback) | ISBN
9781433836954 (ebook)
Subjects: CYAC: Stories in rhyme. | Sportsmanship--Fiction.
Classification: LCC PZ8.3.B779 Fcn 2021 (print) | LCC PZ8.3.B779 (ebook) | DDC [E]--dc23
LC record available at https://lccn.loc.gov/2020042651
LC ebook record available at https://lccn.loc.gov/2020042652

Manufactured in the United States of America
10 9 8 7 6 5 4 3 2 1

A Feel Better Book

for Little
Sports

by Holly Brochmann and Leah Bowen
illustrated by Shirley Ng-Benitez

MAGINATION PRESS · WASHINGTON, DC
American Psychological Association

All over the world,
in all different places,
people of all ages,
genders, and races...

Share a love for SPORTS—
they're so much fun!
Yippee! Hooray!
Your team has won!

Sports bring us together,
our passion unites us.
The thrill of the game
totally excites us!

Sports are terrific
in so many ways.
The list of why
could go on for days!

For one thing sports
are so good for you.
They exercise your body
AND your brain, too!

When your body works harder,
your heart becomes stronger.
Your lungs can breathe better,
your energy lasts longer.

From the running and jumping
to the kicking and throwing—
show me those muscles!
See how they're growing?

Meanwhile your mood
is also improving.
Your brain gets a boost
from all of that moving.

Speaking of brains,
there's so much to learn!
Like how good it feels
to get something you earn.

But remember it's not all
about getting that win.
Sportsmanship matters
just as much in the end.

Have respect for your teammates
and the other side too.

Listen to your coaches
when they're talking to you.

Always be courteous,
considerate, and kind.
You can be still be tough
at the same time!

YOU be the one
when someone falls down
to run over and help them
up from the ground.

And when your team wins,
have compassion and grace.
Treat the winners the same
as the ones in last place.

Go ahead, celebrate!
Cheer with everyone!
It's okay to be proud
of what you have done.

But also remember
those on the losing side.
They're probably feeling
they've lost their pride.

Shake their hands and say,
"thanks for the game."
Next time the score
might not be the same.

But what happens when games don't go *your* way? You're feeling frustrated and don't want to play.

It's a swing! A pass!
A kick and ... a miss!
It's not fun anymore
when sports are like this!

You're losing the game
so you're losing your temper!
You want to throw all your stuff
or yell at a team member.

But that's the thing about sports:
you can't always win.
The excitement of trying
is what keeps you in.

So don't spoil the fun
by losing your head.
When you're feeling frustrated
try this instead…

Step away from the game,
take your own time out.
It's better to pause
than to scream and shout.

Place your hand on your heart,
feel it beat in your chest,
then take several deep breaths
to help with the stress.

You'll begin to calm down
in a minute or two.
Now get back in the game—
your teammates need you!

Finally remember
these feelings won't stay.
Don't let this one game
ruin your day.

So whether playing in a rink,
on the field or the court,
above all remember:
BE A GOOD SPORT!

Reader's Note

Many parents and caregivers introduce their children to competitive sports at an early age these days, and understandably so. Not only do sports offer physical benefits, but they can teach children important lessons such as teamwork and sportsmanship, to name a couple. But while sports are mostly intended for fun among kids so young, these competitions can also produce some BIG emotions when things don't go their way.

A Feel Better Book for Little Sports helps kids navigate their first years of competitive sports by addressing all the great aspects of playing—how good it is for the body and mind, and all the important lessons learned—while also offering tips on how to manage the inevitable, not so fun side of sports—like not playing your best and, of course, losing.

Sports are terrific in so many ways. There is a good chance the majority of children who read this book were exposed to sports before they could even walk. It doesn't matter who you are or where in the world you live, friendly competition is a favorite pastime. Whether a child has attended a sibling's sporting events or simply experienced their family watching a favorite team play on TV, very early on they learn that sports equal excitement. Children also quickly figure out that winning is "good" and losing is "bad." But with a little bit of guidance, kids can discover there's so much more to sports than just winning and losing.

Show me those muscles, see how they're growing? So while succeeding may be the ultimate goal, talk to your kids about all the other benefits sports have to offer, such as what they can do for you physically. Children may notice that athletes often have very strong, healthy-looking bodies. You can help drive this point home by saying things such as, "Soccer players have such strong legs from all the running and kicking!" Or, "Chasing that ball gives her so much energy!"

Your brain gets a boost from all of that moving. Adults know that physical activity can help improve your mood, but let your child know that, too! Sports are a great way to teach them about endorphins and how movement can help lower stress, enhance clear thinking, improve confidence, and even help you sleep better!

But remember it's not all about getting that win. Remind your kids that sports do so much for the world. They bring people together peacefully in friendly competition. They give people something to cheer for, to look forward to, to get excited about. And sports teach valuable lessons in kindness, sportsmanship, and respect for your teammates as well as the opposition. The key is to offer these reminders at the right time, like while watching the Olympics or reading this book. The information probably won't be as well-received if you bring this up to your child fresh off a tough loss.

You can be still be tough at the same time! It is also important to teach your children how feelings and behaviors are not mutually exclusive. Showing grace and kindness (helping a person from the opposite team up from the ground) does not mean that you are not a tough or competitive player. You can be both! A good way to teach this is by demonstrating through example. Cheer on your child's team and talk through the strategy and methods for winning the game. But also model friendly, supportive behaviors toward the opposing team. For instance, you can acknowledge another child's performance by saying to their parents after the game, "Congratulations on the win—your daughter scored a great goal at the end!" You can also point out positive, sportsmanlike actions you saw from your child during a game. For example, you can say, "What a great goal you had today! That was awesome! I also liked how you smiled and said hello to the kid on the Avengers team. That was so nice!" It also goes without saying that as a parent, your attitude toward the game is important. Focusing on the positive and exhibiting kindness towards everyone involved will help your child have a positive attitude as well.

It's okay to be proud of what you have done. Winning is fun and it feels good! It's okay to celebrate! Just help your child learn how to celebrate respectfully. Although technically the meaning might be the same, there is a big difference between saying "We won!" and "You lost!" Remind your child to focus on what they and their team did well, as opposed to what the other team didn't do.

But what happens when games don't go your way? Losing or not performing your best is inevitable. This is especially tough for really young kids whose caregivers have been working to boost their confidence with steady praise and encouragement. Competitive sports often give children their first experience with loss, and tempers can happen as a result of these feelings of disappointment and frustration. You do not need to discount these feelings—it IS disappointing when you lose! Something you might say is "I know you wanted to win. You tried your best and you're sad it didn't go the way you wanted." It can be as simple as that. Not every moment is a teaching moment. Sometimes the best thing you can do is acknowledge your child's feelings and just show that you get it.

You can also focus on any positives that you saw. For example, you could say something like, "One thing I saw you do during the game was dribble the ball between your legs—I know you've been working on that!" Emphasizing personal growth and goals gives the child more control of how they view the outcome and, while they will most likely be disappointed in the overall result, they will learn to balance those feelings with a sense of pride for what they personally accomplished.

Step away from the game, take your own time out. When frustrations and resulting emotions start to interfere, just taking a break can be so helpful. One suggestion is to come up with a special phrase you can propose to your little one that represents a personal timeout, like "Let's take a quick Blake Break," or "How about a really fast Tina Timeout?" Children also seem to respond to "call backs" that are often used in both school and sports. Perhaps you could also try something like "One, two, three! What do you see?" Then run through a quick grounding activity and discuss the blue sky, the green grass, the smells of the gym, the cold ice, etc. Basically, just pick one of the five senses and do a simple mindfulness activity to regroup.

Then take several deep breaths to help with the stress. Never underestimate this proven strategy to help in special times. Your kids (and worked-up parents, too) just need reminders of this. Have a "deep breath" signal you can wave from the audience, or hand out pinwheels during team time-outs to help everyone breathe deep, blow out their frustration to make their pinwheels spin, and regain composure.

Above all remember BE A GOOD SPORT! Unsportsmanlike conduct happens at all levels of sports, and kids will witness this. But they'll also see acts of kindness—an NFL player helping a player from the opposite team to his feet after a tackle, the second place gymnast hugging and congratulating the gymnast who comes in first. Point these out and offer examples of how your child can exhibit this behavior in their own competitions, then commend them when they do!

But it's most important to remember that your attitude will influence your child's attitude about the game. Whether your child wins or loses, acknowledge the effort that was made. "You played so hard today and never gave up!" "You're disappointed you didn't win and are worried you did not play your best." "You're so proud of all your goals! You felt so strong out there!" Your job, at this stage in a child's development, is to foster the love of sports, encourage respectful play, and reinforce the feeling of accomplishment. So it is not necessary to offer critical analysis of what you feel they did wrong. Chances are, they already know it. Well-intentioned parents have found themselves putting too much pressure on their children. Especially at the beginning ages for sports, encouraging effort, boosting self-esteem, and exercising the mind and body are what's important. Kids have enough stress these days, so let's try and remember as the parents and caregivers to offer support by listening, encouraging resiliency, and helping your child continue to love and learn from their sport.

About the Authors

Sisters **Leah Bowen** and **Holly Brochmann** are dedicated wives, mothers, and authors, each passionate about contributing to a mentally and emotionally healthier society in a meaningful way. Leah has a master of education degree in counseling with a focus in play therapy. She is a licensed professional counselor and registered play therapist in the state of Texas where she currently practices, and she is committed to helping her child clients work through issues including trauma, depression, and anxiety. Holly has a degree in journalism and enjoys creative writing both as a hobby and as a primary part of her career in public relations. This is the sisters' fifth book in the Feel Better Books for Little Kids series published by Magination Press. Both sisters live in Texas. Visit them at bsistersbooks.com and on Twitter and Instagram @bsistersbooks.

About the Illustrator

Shirley Ng-Benitez, an award-winning illustrator, is honored to illustrate the entire Feel Better Books for Little Kids series. She lives with her family and two black cats, Miso & Luna, in the San Francisco Bay Area. She is currently writing and illustrating stories for children. Visit shirleyngbenitez.com and @shirleysillos on Twitter and Instagram.